Elizabeti's Doll

by STEPHANIE STUVE-BODEEN

illustrated by CHRISTY HALE

LEE & LOW BOOKS INC. • New York

Text copyright © 1998 by Stephanie Stuve-Bodeen

Illustrations copyright © 1998 by Christy Hale

All rights reserved. No part of the contents of this book may be reproduced
by any means without the written permission of the publisher.

LEE & LOW BOOKS Inc., 95 Madison Avenue, New York, NY 10016.

leeandlow.com

Manufactured in China by RR Donnelley

Book Design by Christy Hale

Book Production by The Kids at Our House

The text is set in Octavian.

The illustrations are rendered in mixed media.

(HC) 15 14 13 12 11 10 9 8

(PB) 25 24 23 22 21

First Edition

Library of Congress Cataloging-in-Publication Data

Stuve-Bodeen, Stephanie

Elizabeti's doll/by Stephanie Stuve-Bodeen ; illustrated by Christy Hale.—1st ed.

p. cm.

Summary: When a young Tanzanian girl gets a new baby brother, she finds a rock,
which she names Eva, and makes it her baby doll.

ISBN 978-1-880000-70-0 (hardcover)   ISBN 978-1-58430-081-6 (paperback)

[1. Dolls—Fiction. 2. Rocks—Fiction. 3. Tanzania—Fiction.] I. Hale, Christy, ill.
II. Title.

PZ7.S9418E1 1998

[E]—dc21   98-13086   CIP AC

MIX
Paper from
responsible sources
FSC® C144853

For Tim, Bee, and Tangelo.

Asante sana to Bobbi and the village of Malula—S.S.B.

For Elizabeth Humphreys, my dear Betsy, with love, friendship,
and fond memories of our doll days—C.H.

Elizabeti had a new baby brother named Obedi. Elizabeti watched Mama take care of him and she wanted to care for her own baby.

She didn't have a doll, so she went outside and picked up a stick.
She tried to hug it, but it poked her and she dropped it on the ground.

Then Elizabeti picked up a rock. It was just the right size to hold and it
didn't poke Elizabeti when she hugged it. She kissed the rock and named it Eva.

When baby Obedi had a bath, he splashed and got Mama wet.

When Eva had a bath, she behaved very nicely and only splashed a little.

Mama fed Obedi and he gave a loud "Brrrrp!"
Elizabeti fed Eva, but she was too polite to burp.

Mama changed the cloth wrapped around Obedi's bottom and it was very messy!

Elizabeti was very relieved to find that Eva's bottom was still clean.

When Mama did her chores, she tied Obedi onto her back
with a bright cloth called a kanga.

When Elizabeti did her chores, she also tied Eva onto her back
with a kanga. Mama had to help a little.

Elizabeti went to visit her friend Rahaili. Rahaili laughed
when she saw that Elizabeti had a rock for a doll.

But Rahaili didn't have a doll either, so when Elizabeti left,
Rahaili found her own rock and named it Malucey.

When Elizabeti got home, it was time for her to get water from the village well. She took Eva out of the kanga and laid her on the ground near some other rocks, so she wouldn't be lonely.

Then Elizabeti wrapped the kanga into a small bundle, put it
on top of her head, and placed the water jug on top of the kanga.
This was how she always carried water and other heavy things.

Elizabeti soon returned with the water and took it to her sister Pendo inside the cooking hut where all the family's meals were made.

Then Elizabeti ran outside to get Eva. But Eva was gone!
Elizabeti looked all around, but she couldn't find Eva.

Mama found a new rock and gave it to Elizabeti. Elizabeti shook
her head when she saw it. The rock was just a rock.

Pendo also brought Elizabeti a rock, but it wasn't Eva either.

Elizabeti was very sad and sat quietly until it was time
to help Pendo in the cooking hut.

The family had rice for dinner every night, and it was Elizabeti's job to
put the pot of rice on the fire pit, which was made of three large stones.

Elizabeti sadly filled the pot with water and set it on the stones to boil. But one of the stones wasn't a stone at all. It was Eva!

Elizabeti called for Mama and together they moved the pot of
water and rolled Eva away from the fire. Although Eva was a bit
dirty, she hadn't been hurt.

Pendo ran outside to get a new stone for the fire pit, which is just how poor Eva had become lost.

Eva sat quietly while Elizabeti cleaned her off and hugged her.

At bedtime, Mama sang a lullaby and rocked Obedi in her arms until he fell asleep. Elizabeti sang a lullaby too, but she fell asleep before Eva did.

Mama covered Elizabeti and Eva with a blanket. She smiled and thought that, one day, Elizabeti would make a fine mother. Eva thought so too.